to Nora,
Dream Big!
Jody Mackey ♡

Sally Loves...®

to Dance!

Written and Illustrated by

Jody Mackey

Sally Loves . . . ® to Dance!: The compilation and subject, the format, design,
layout, and coloring used in this book are trademarks and/or trade dress of
Jody L. Mackey and Champ Youth, Inc.

This book may be ordered directly from the publisher, however, please try
your local bookstore first. Call us at 1 (855) 529-2403 or see our full line of
products promoting active lifestyles and building confidence, for children at:

Website
www.champyouth.com
Published by Champ Youth, Inc

This is a work of fiction. Names, characters, places and incidents either
are the product of the author's imagination or are used fictitiously, and
any resemblance to actual persons, living or dead, events, or locales is
entirely coincidental.

Rev. date 10/25/2014
Second Edition 11/16/2016

To order additional copies of this book, contact

Champ Youth, Inc
P.O. Box 35250 Tucson,
AZ, 85740 1-855-529-2403
www.champyouth.com

To Helenjoyce, you are very precious to me. My book, *Sally Loves . . . to Dance!* is a celebration of you. Your loyalty and friendship are the most generous gifts I have ever received. Thank you. ♥

May all your dreams come true.

Sally loves to dance.

Sally likes ballet.

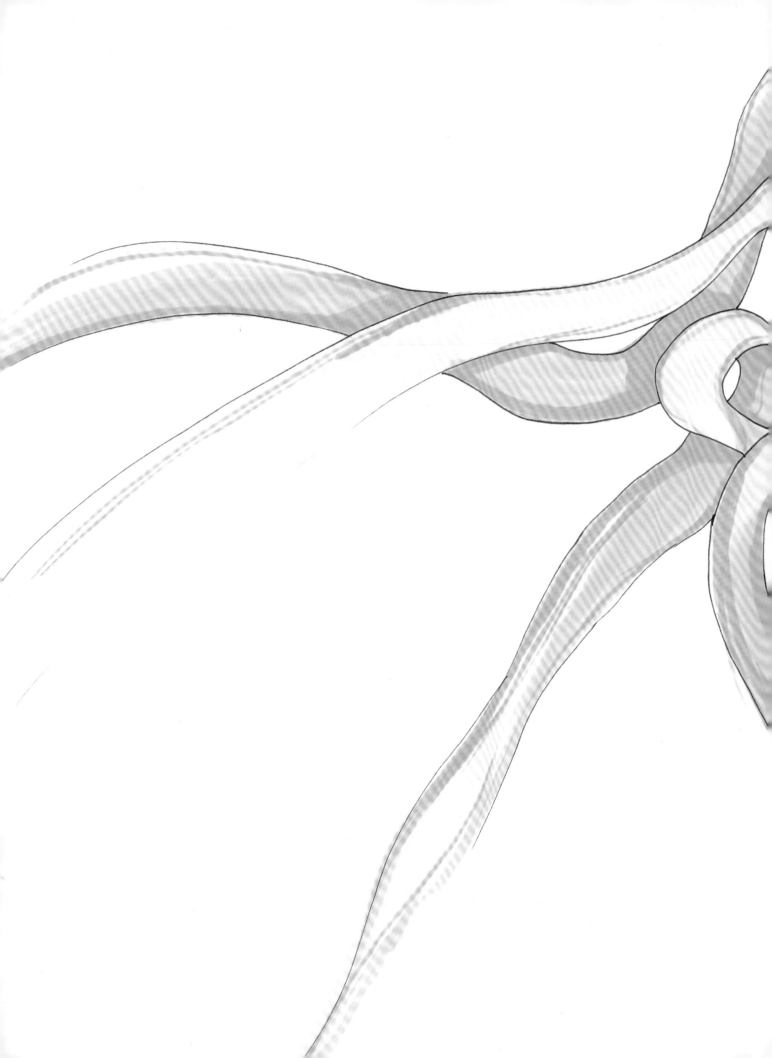

Sally has pink ballet shoes
and she takes ballet lessons.

Sally likes jazz dance. She likes tap, hip hop, and disco dance. Sally even likes to folk dance.

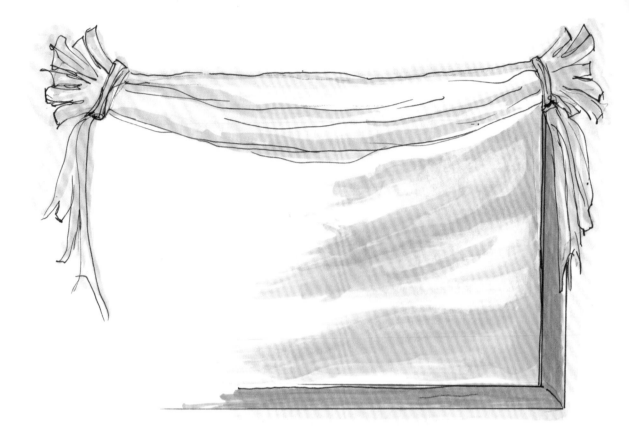

But Sally likes **hula dancing**
most of all.

Sally's friend Evangelyne hula dances.
Evangelyne dances onstage with her sisters
at luaus.

(Luau "A Hawaiian feast or party usually accompanied
by traditional Hawaiian music and dance")

Evangelyne's grandma is a Grand
Kumu Hula and plans the luaus.

(Kumu Hula "Hula teacher")

"Sally, will you dance with my sisters
and me at the Hawaiian festival?"
asks Evangelyne.

A little hesitant, Sally replies, "Could I?
I love to dance."

"Imagine how fun it will be. My grandma will teach us the hula dances. We can put flowers in our hair and wear beautiful dresses," says Evangelyne.

While Sally's mom takes time to brush and style her hair, Sally wonders if she could ever dance as beautifully as Evangelyne and her sisters. "Mom, do you really think I can dance onstage

in the luau?" Sally asks.

"Honey, if you can dream it and if you work hard at it, you can do anything you

set your mind to," replies Sally's mom.

Sally's eyes gleam as the words of

encouragement unfold in her head, she says to

herself, "I am going to work hard—

I love to dance."

Sally starts taking hula lessons once a week. She practices hula dancing each day after school. Sally dances with Evangelyne and her sisters every weekend she can.

Sometimes, She dances with her dog, Little Mack. She even puts flowers in his hair!

One day, Evangelyne's grandma
gives Sally the most beautiful
dress, softly adorned with pink satin
ribbons, along with flowers to put in her hair.

Sally is going to be onstage
in the luau.

It's finally here . . . Saturday, the day of the
luau. Sally's whole family is going, Sally's mom,
her dad, and even her brother, Ryan, are
attending the performance.

Bubbling with anticipation, Sally dresses and
gets ready early. She even has some extra time to
enjoy with her family. Ryan asks, "Will there
be food at the luau?"

Sally giggles, "Oh Ryan, of course there will,
it's a luau." she says, as she gets an encouraging
hug from her mom and dad.

With time only for a brief last minute check of their flowers and bows, Evangelyne asks Sally, "Are you ready?"

Feeling a fluttering in her tummy, "I'm a little nervous," she replies.

Sally lets out a long sigh as she thinks of the dance steps in her head, then says to Evangelyne, "You are such a great dancer."

"Don't worry Sally, we know all the dances, you are a great dancer too," says Evangelyne.

As they walk to the stage, the friends say to each other, "Remember to smile . . . aloha!"

(Aloha "Expressing love and affection, peace, compassion – also used to say goodbye and hello")

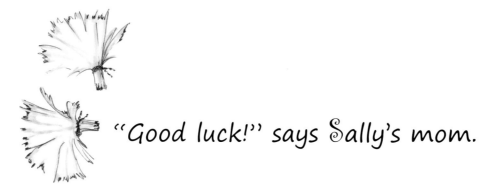

"Good luck!" says Sally's mom.

"Have fun!" says Sally's dad.

"ALOHA," shouts Ryan.

The stage lights up and the music begins to play. The luau performance is starting.

Sally dances, she points her toes . . . heels up, toes down. Sally twirls, Sally spins, and she reaches her arms to the sky, all in perfect unison with Evangelyne and her sisters.

The dance tells a story of the sun shining upon the ocean shore—beautiful as the blue sky dancing on the water.

When the dance is over, Sally and
Evangelyne hug each other tight.

Now wishing the dance had not yet ended,
a blissful Sally says, "Dancing is
so much fun, this is the best day ever!"

"There is no one I would rather dance
with than you. Mahalo," the friends say
to each other.

(Mahalo "Expressing thanks, gratitude; to thank")

Sally Loves. . . you!